This book belongs to...

This is the first book of mine where my slightly silly name is printed large on the cover and glitters like gold. There's a certain grandness about the idea of a Treasury, that suggests keeping it for best. But what any author really wants is for his work to become dog-eared and familiar.

Children's authors are particularly blessed in this regard; their readers can give a book doggy ears in no time at all. I hope that's what will happen to these four stories.

Mick Inkpen

The
MICK
INKPEN
Treasury

Lullabyhullaballoo!

Nothing

Bear

Billy's Beetle

h

*Hodder
Children's
Books*

A division of Hodder Headline Limited

Lullabyhullaballoo!

The sun is down.
The moon is up.
It is bedtime for the
Little Princess.
But outside the castle…

A dragon is roaring.
What shall we do?
He's hissing and snorting!
What shall we do?
We'll tell him to SSSH!
That's what we'll do.

SSSH!

But,

The brave knights are clanking.
What shall we do?
They're rattling and clunking!
What shall we do?
We'll tell them to SSSH!
That's what we'll do.

SSSH!

But,
The ghosts are oooooing.
What shall we do?
They're ooo ooo ooooooing!
What shall we do?
We'll tell them to SSSH!
That's what we'll do.

SSSH!

But,

The giant is stamping.

What shall we do?

He's galumphing and stomping!

What shall we do?

We'll tell him to SSSH!

That's what we'll do.

SSSH!

B ut,
  Out in the forest
      Wolves are howling
  Owls are hooting
      Frogs are croaking
  Mice are squeaking
      Bats are flapping
  Bears are growling

...STOP!

Now the Princess is smiling.

Her eyelids are drooping.

The Princess is sleeping.

So what shall we do?
We'll tiptoe to bed
And we shall sleep too.
We shall sleep too.

But,

Nothing

Anew baby is on the way.
The family are moving out of Number
47 to a bigger house round the corner.
The cat has gone missing. But
everything else is packed and ready
to go.

Nothing has been left behind…

The little thing in the attic at
Number 47 had forgotten all about
daylight. It had been squashed in the
dark for so long that it could remember
very little of anything. Stuck beneath
years of junk, it could not recall how it
felt to stand up, or to stretch out its arms.
So long had it been there, even its own
name was lost.

'I wonder who I am,'
it thought. But it
could not remember.

The day came when the family that
lived at Number 47 were to move.

All day long the little thing listened
to thuds and thumps and the sound of
tramping feet in the house below,
until at last the attic door was flung open
and large hands began
to stuff cardboard
boxes full
of junk.

The little thing felt the weight on top
of it gradually lighten, and suddenly the
glare of a torch beam stung its eyes.

'What have we got here?' said a voice.

'Oh, it's nothing,' said another. 'Let the
new people get rid of it.'

The torch was switched off. The boxes
were carried out. And moments later,
somewhere down below, the front door
slammed shut. Number 47
was empty.

'So that's my name,'
thought the little thing.
'Nothing!'

For the first time in a very long time, Nothing sat up. He looked around him at the cobwebs and shafts of dusty moonlight. Then, in the quiet, he heard the patter of feet and a mouse came running towards him.

'New People always try to get rid of you,' it said, without introducing itself. It looked at him. 'Seen you under the rug. What are you?'

'Nothing,' replied Nothing.

'Well, nothing or not, you can't stay here, not with New People coming,' said the mouse. It hurried off.

Nothing struggled to his feet. On unsteady legs he followed the dusty paw prints. The mouse stopped by a moonlit gap under the eaves.

'Through there,' it said. 'Good luck!'

With a wriggle of its tail it disappeared under the floorboards.

'I used to have a tail!' thought Nothing suddenly.
He felt sure of it.

How do you think you would feel if you had been squashed in the dark for years and years. And then you squeezed through a tiny hole to find yourself under the big, starry sky?

Well, there are no words for that kind of feeling, so I won't try to tell you how Nothing felt, except to say that he sat on the roof staring up at the moon and stars for a very long time.

He was still staring upwards as he made his way along the gutter, which is why he fell straight down the drainpipe!

Nothing rolled into the garden and sat up.

'What on earth are you?' said a silky voice. The fox, for that is what it was, left the dustbin and trotted towards him.

'I'm Nothing,' said Nothing.

The fox sniffed at him. Its whiskers quivered. Its ears pricked.

'I used to have ears and whiskers!' thought Nothing suddenly. He was sure of it.

The fox spoke again. 'Nothing,' it said disdainfully. 'Nothing worth eating, that's for sure.' It trotted away silently.

Nothing wandered into the garden and came across a lily pond. There a frog sat gently croaking. As Nothing approached it plopped into the water and, with a kick of its stripy legs, it disappeared from view.

'I used to have stripes!' thought Nothing. 'I'm sure I did!'

The ripples cleared and Nothing found himself staring at his own reflection. It was odd. It was ugly.

'What are you?' it said to Nothing sadly. A tear rolled up its face and splashed onto the surface of the pond. The ugly face disappeared among the ripples.

'What are you?' repeated Nothing.

'I'm a cat!' said a loud voice. 'Who's asking?'
A big, lolloping tabby cat tumbled out from
behind a bush, and grinned at Nothing.

Nothing opened his mouth to explain that
he had been talking to himself, and that he did
not know what he was, and that
he was lost, and that he had
just been sniffed by a
horrible fox, and that he
was feeling very miserable.
But instead he found himself
shuddering and shaking, as great uncontrollable
sobs quivered up his little, raggedy body and sat
him on the ground.

'I don't know who I am!' he howled. 'I don't
know who I am!'

The cat licked him full in the face.

After a while
Nothing stopped crying.
The cat lay down
beside him. Between
Nothing's loud sniffs it told him all about
itself. How its name was Toby. And how it
came from a long line of Tobys.

'I live in the house,' it said. 'At least I
used to. We moved round the corner
today. They think I'm lost. But it's all the
same to me. Number 47, Number 97,
what's the difference? It's all my patch.
D'you want to see?'

Nothing sniffed once more and
nodded.

'Course you do!' said the cat.
It picked up Nothing and sprang
onto the garden wall.

Nothing had never ridden
through the night in a cat's mouth before.
It whisked him up through the branches of a
tree and out onto the rooftops, where they
sped along, with the moon racing them
behind the chimney pots.

'I'm taking you the long way round,'
panted the cat. 'It's more fun!'

All the while, joggling along inside Nothing's
head, there was a thought trying to get out. It
felt like an important thought. It had something
to do with the cat.

The cat jumped the fence at Number 97 and
trotted in through the back door. He found an
old man dozing in a chair surrounded by
unpacked boxes.

'That's Grandpa,' whispered the cat to
Nothing, and dropped him on the old man's lap.

'So there you are!' said Grandpa waking up.
'What have you brought me this time?' He put
on his glasses and looked at Nothing.
'Good heavens! Look everyone! Look what
Toby's found!'

Nothing looked up at Grandpa
and saw a face he knew.
The important thought inside
his head popped open like
a jack-in-a-box.

The family gathered round to look.

'What is it, Grandpa?' said the children. But Grandpa was busy rummaging among the cardboard boxes.

'I know it's here somewhere,' he said. 'Ah, there it is!'

He pulled out an old photograph album and opened it, turning the pages until he came to a fading photograph of a baby.

'That's me!' he said. 'And that's Toby's Great Great Great Great Grandfather. And this,' he said, tapping the photograph and tickling Nothing's tummy with his forefinger, 'this is Little Toby!'

At last Nothing remembered who he was. Though he had no ears, nor whiskers, no tail and no stripes, he was for certain a little cloth tabby cat whose name was not Nothing, but Little Toby.

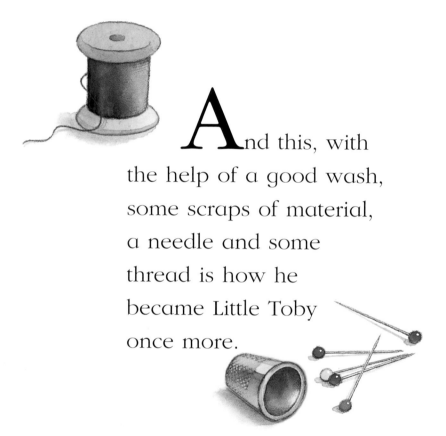

And this, with
the help of a good wash,
some scraps of material,
a needle and some
thread is how he
became Little Toby
once more.

When the new baby arrived, Little Toby
was handed back to Grandpa who tucked him
carefully in the cot.

And, straight away, the new baby began to
chew on his ear, which if it had been your ear would
probably have hurt a little, but since it belonged
to a little cloth cat, did not hurt in the slightest.

Bear

A small whooshing sound.
Then a plop!
A bounce.
And a kind of squeak.
That was how the bear landed
in my baby sister's playpen.

Have you ever had a bear fall out of the sky, right in front of you? At first I thought he was a teddy bear. He just lay there, crumpled on the quilt.

Then he got up and took Sophie's drink. And her biscuit. That's when I knew he was real.

The bear climbed out of the playpen
and looked at me.

He rolled on his back, lifted his
paws and growled.
He seemed to
want to play.

I put him in
Sophie's baby bouncer.
He was very good at bouncing,
much better than Sophie.

I sneaked the bear into the house under the quilt. At bedtime I hid him among my toys.

'Don't you say anything, Sophie!' I said. 'I want to keep this bear.'

Sophie doesn't say much anyway. She isn't even two yet.

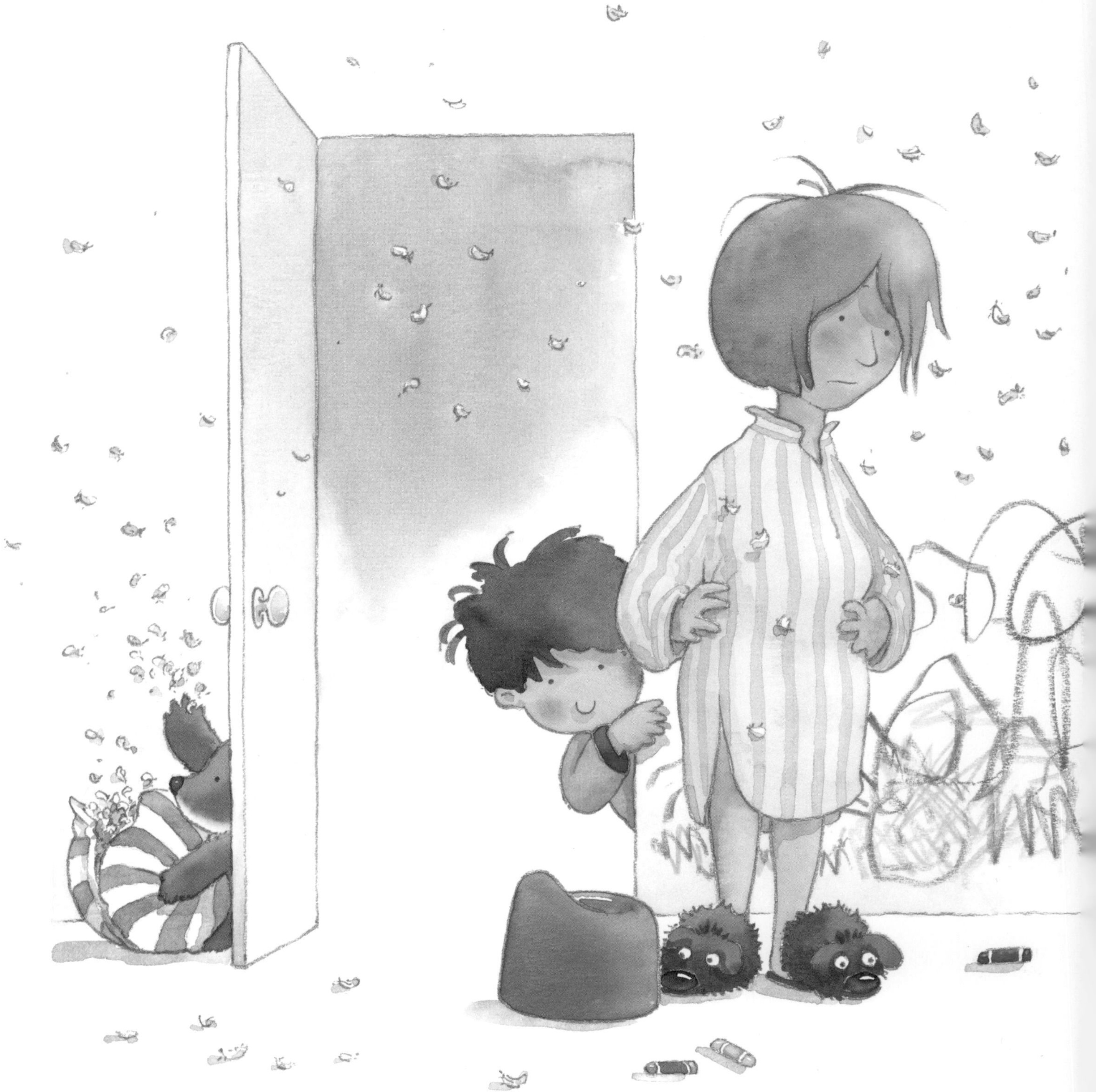

In the morning the sound of shouting woke me up.

'Sophie, that's naughty! It was Mum. She was looking at the feathers.

'Sophie! That's very naughty!' She was looking at the scribble. Then she looked at the potty.

'Sophie!' she said. 'Good girl!'

But I don't think it was Sophie.

I'm sure it wasn't Sophie. It definitely wasn't Sophie.

I took the bear to
school in my rucksack.
Everyone wanted to be
my friend.
'Does he bite?' they said.
'He doesn't bite me,'
I said.
'What's his name?'
they said.
'He doesn't
have one.'

We kept him quiet all day
feeding him our lunches. He liked
the peanut butter sandwiches best.

After school, my friends came to
the house.

'Where is he?' they said.

We played with the bear
behind the garage.

We made a
tunnel…

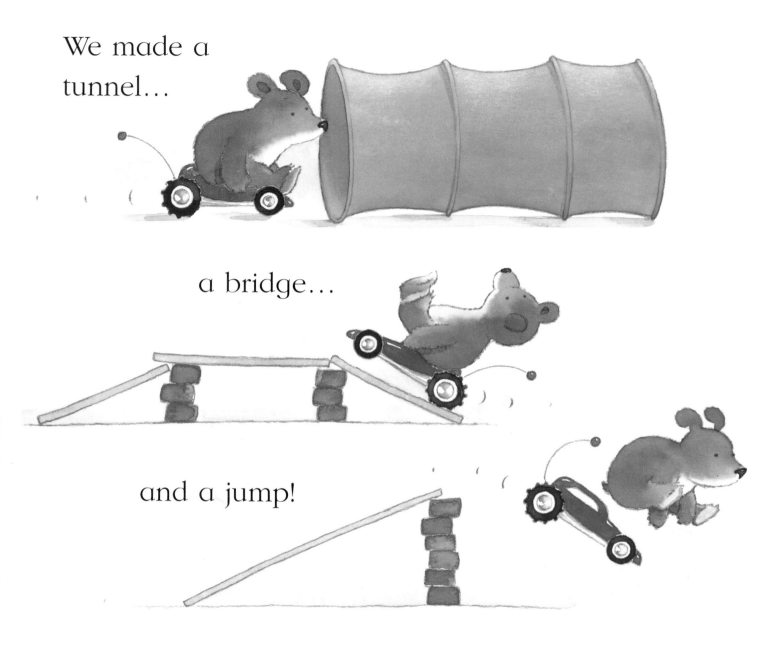

a bridge…

and a jump!

When the car came back the bear
had gone. We looked and looked
but there was no bear anywhere.

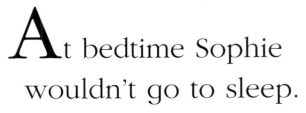

At bedtime Sophie
wouldn't go to sleep.

She didn't want her elephant.
She didn't want her rabbit.
She threw them out of the cot.

I gave her my second best pig.
She threw it out.

'Sophie! That's naughty!'
said Mum.

But Sophie just howled.
She wanted the bear.

CRASH! BANG!
It was the middle
of the night.
SMASH! CLANG!
The noise was coming from
the kitchen. We crept downstairs
and peeped through the door.
It wasn't a burglar.

'Bear!' said Sophie. 'Naughty!'

So today a serious man in a serious hat came to look at our bear. He wrote something in a big black book.

'Will you have to take him away?' I said.

'We nearly always do,' said the man. He pointed his pen at my bear. 'But,' he said, 'this bear is an Exception.'

'This bear,' he went on, 'has fallen quite unexpectedly into a storybook. And it is not up to me to say what should happen next.'

'So can we keep him?' I said.

'Ask them,' he said. And he
pointed straight out of the picture
at YOU!

And you thought for a moment.
You looked at the man.
You looked at the bear.
You looked at Sophie.
You looked at me.

And then you said...

'YES YOU CAN!'

So we did.

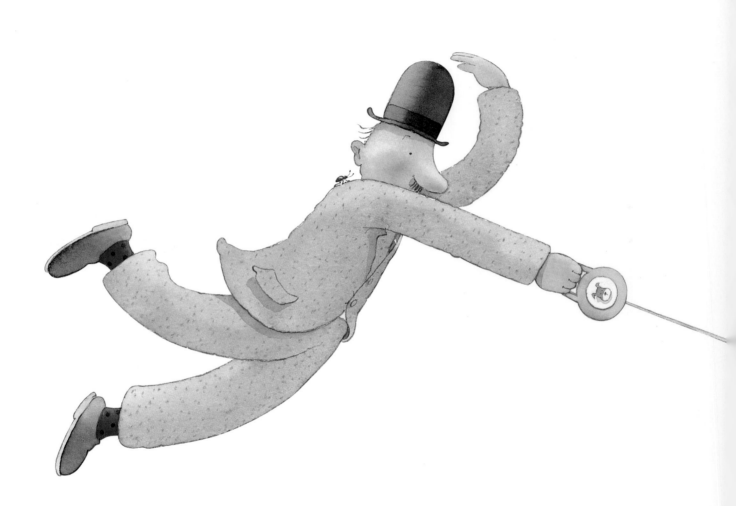

Billy's Beetle

Billy had a beetle in a matchbox.
Or rather he hadn't. He had lost it.
Silly Billy.

'Have you seen my beetle?' he asked
the girl. But she hadn't.

Along came a man with a sniffy dog.

'Don't you worry!' said the man with the sniffy dog. 'My sniffy dog will soon find your beetle!'

Off went the sniffy dog.

Sniff.Sniff.Sniff.

Soon the sniffy dog had found a hedgehog,
two spiders, some worms and a bone.
But not the beetle.

'I will help find Billy's beetle,' said the
hedgehog. And so the search continued.

Suddenly, the sniffy dog stopped digging
and took off like a rocket!

'Look at him go!' said the man.

'He can smell Billy's beetle!'

But the sniffy dog had not smelled Billy's beetle.
He had smelled sausages.

'Leave, sniffy dog! Leave!' said the man.
So the sniffy dog grabbed the sausages,
and left!

Now there was Billy, the girl, the hedgehog,
the sniffy dog, the man with the sniffy dog,
and the woman without the sausages,
all looking for Billy's beetle.
(And a polar bear who had joined in for fun.)

The sniffy dog found a tuba. It belonged to a man in an oompah band.

'I don't think Billy's beetle is in there,' said the bandsman. 'But we will help you look.'

So the oompah band played and off they went again. Oompah! Oompah! Sniff, sniff, sniff!

An elephant wandered over to see what all
the fuss was about.

'Stand aside!' said the man with the sniffy dog.
'My sniffy dog is looking for this boy's beetle!'
The elephant became very excited.

'I've seen it!' he said.

The elephant jumped up and down and pointed
with his trunk.

'Is THAT the beetle?' he trumpeted triumphantly.

'No,' said Billy. 'That is not my beetle.
That is a furry caterpillar.'

Instantly the elephant was untriumphant and untrumpetible. He sat down.

The girl sighed a long, long sigh and sat down too.

'Where can it be?' she said.

The man with the sniffy dog, the sniffy dog, the lady without the sausages, the polar bear and the oompah band sat down next to them.

But the hedgehog was hopping from one foot to the other, and pointing.

'The beetle! It's the beetle!' he squeaked.

'We've found the beetle! We've found the beetle!'
'HOORAY! HOORAY! HOORAY!' they shouted.

'BUT WHERE IS BILLY?' said the girl.
Everybody stopped shouting. They looked up.
They looked down. They looked behind, in front,
and in between. But Billy had disappeared.

'Don't you worry!' said the man with the
sniffy dog. 'My sniffy dog has found something!'

But the sniffy dog had not found Billy.
He had found a little pig.

　'Excuse me,' said the little pig.
'I have lost my furry caterpillar.
Have you seen him?'

So the girl, the sniffy dog, the man with the
sniffy dog, the hedgehog, the woman without the
sausages, the polar bear, the oompah band,
the elephant, the little pig AND the beetle
all went off together to look for Billy
and the furry caterpillar.

And once again
it was the hedgehog
who found them...

...and the sniffy dog who didn't!